FARMINGTON COMMUNITY LIBRARY

IN MEMORY OF:
SHIRLEY MARTIN

GIVEN BY:
HARVEY & PAMELA VANNORMAN

GOOD NIGHT, GORILLA

Peggy Rathmann

PUFFIN BOOKS

**For Mr. and Mrs. Joseph McQuaid,
and all their little gorillas**

PUFFIN BOOKS
Published by the Penguin Group
Penguin Putnam Books for Young Readers, 345 Hudson Street, New York, New York 10014, U.S.A.
Penguin Books Ltd, 27 Wrights Lane, London W8 5TZ, England
Penguin Books Australia Ltd, Ringwood, Victoria, Australia
Penguin Books Canada Ltd, 10 Alcorn Avenue, Toronto, Ontario, Canada M4V 3B2
Penguin Books (N.Z.) Ltd, 182-190 Wairau Road, Auckland 10, New Zealand

Penguin Books Ltd, Registered Offices: Harmondsworth, Middlesex, England

First published in the United States of America by G. P. Putnam's Sons, a division of The Putnam & Grosset Group, 1994
Published by Puffin Books, a division of Penguin Putnam Books for Young Readers, 2000

24 26 28 30 29 27 25

THE LIBRARY OF CONGRESS HAS CATALOGED THE G. P. PUTNAM'S SONS EDITION AS FOLLOWS:
Rathmann, Peggy. Good night, Gorilla/Peggy Rathmann. p. cm.
Summary: An unobservant zookeeper is followed home by all the animals he thinks he has left behind in the zoo.
[1. Zoo animals—Fiction. 2. Zoos—Fiction.] I. Title.
PZ7.R1936Go 1994 92-29020 CIP AC [E]—dc20
ISBN 0-399-22445-9

This edition ISBN 978-0-698-11649-8

Printed in the United States of America